Chimpanzees for TEA!

by

Jo Empson

Philomel Books

"Hey, Vincent!

This cupboard is looking a bit bare.

Can you rush to the shops . . .

. . . and get:

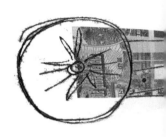

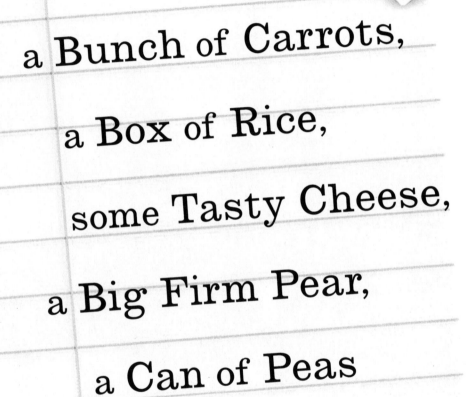

a Bunch of Carrots,

a Box of Rice,

some Tasty Cheese,

a Big Firm Pear,

a Can of Peas

and hurry home in time for tea!"

Sorry, can't stop, Mr. Singh.
I've got to rush to the shops and get . . .
a Bunch of Carrots, a Box of Rice,
some Tasty Cheese, a Big Firm Pear, a Can of Peas

and hurry home in time for tea. BUT . . .

Oh NO... the

list!

What was it? Umm . . . a Bunch of Carrots . . . errr . . .

a Box of Rice, some Tasty Cheese . . . a Big Firm Pear . . .

... a **Trapeze** and hurry home in time for tea.

... I've got to rush to the shops and get a Bunch

of Carrots, a Box of Rice, some Tasty Cheese . . . .

aaaa . . .

aaaa . . .

aaaand . . .

. . . some Chimpanzees, a Big Furry

Bear, a Trapeze . . .

and hurry home
in time for tea.

rush to the shops and get a Bunch of Carrots . . .

... a **Box** of **Mice**, some Chimpanzees, a Big Furry Bear, a Trapeze and hurry home in time for tea.

. . . a Branch of Parrots,

a Box of Mice, some Chimpanzees,

a Big Furry Bear, a Trapeze. Hurry home and . . .

. . . invite

them ALL in for . . .

...tea!

For John with love & thanks — J.E.

PHILOMEL BOOKS
an imprint of Penguin Random House LLC
375 Hudson Street, New York, NY 10014

Copyright © 2016 by Jo Empson.
First American edition published in 2016 by Philomel Books.
Published in Great Britain by Penguin Random House (UK) in 2016.
Penguin supports copyright. Copyright fuels creativity, encourages diverse
voices, promotes free speech, and creates a vibrant culture. Thank you for
buying an authorized edition of this book and for complying with copyright laws by not
reproducing, scanning, or distributing any part of it in any form without permission. You are
supporting writers and allowing Penguin to continue to publish books for every reader.

Philomel Books is a registered trademark of Penguin Random House LLC.

Library of Congress Cataloging-in-Publication Data is available upon request.
Manufactured in China by RR Donnelley Asia Printing Solutions Ltd.
ISBN 978-1-101-99621-8
Special Markets ISBN 978-1-524-73876-1 Not for resale
10 9 8 7 6 5 4 3 2 1

Text set in New Clarendon MT Std. The art was done in watercolor.

This Imagination Library edition is published by Penguin Young Readers, a division
of Penguin Random House, exclusively for Dolly Parton's Imagination Library,
a not-for-profit program designed to inspire a love of reading and learning, sponsored
in part by The Dollywood Foundation. Penguin's trade editions of this work are
available wherever books are sold.